Murals for Joy

by Veronica Freeman Ellis
illustrated by Colin Bootman

 HOUGHTON MIFFLIN   BOSTON

Celia and her mother, Mrs. Delaney, lived in the city. Every summer Celia visited her cousin Joy. Joy lived near the seashore with her parents.

When Celia visited, the girls played on the beach and swam. Sometimes they went sailing with Joy's parents.

This summer was different. Joy was
spending four weeks with Celia in the city.

The girls sat outside Celia's apartment
building.

"Is sitting on the steps all you do?"
asked Joy.

"No," answered Celia, "but it's fun
watching people."

"I don't think it's fun," grumbled Joy. "If we were at my house, we'd be swimming, or we'd be sailing around the bay."

"City people do different things for fun," said Celia. "After four weeks, you may like what we do."

"Maybe I will," said Joy. "Or maybe I won't."

The next day the girls went to the Youth Center. "This is my cousin," Celia told the other children. "She'll be coming to the center with me this summer."

The group leader, Ms. Howard, invited Joy to join them in the day's activities.

Ms. Howard told the children they would be talking about important African Americans. Later they would make posters of the people they liked and wanted to learn more about.

In the afternoon Ms. Howard helped the children make sweet potato pie. They ate the pie at snack time.

"Mmmmmm," said Joy. "This pie is dee-licious!"

That evening Mrs. Delaney asked, "Joy, did you have some fun?"

"Not much," mumbled Joy. "I'd have more fun at home."

"Why don't you take her back home, Mom?" asked Celia.

"Give her time," said Mrs. Delaney. "I know she'll like the city."

"Maybe I will," said Joy. "Or maybe I won't."

The next day, Ms. Howard talked about
Frederick Douglass, who fought slavery. She
also talked about the musicians Duke Ellington
and Wynton Marsalis and the writer Toni
Morrison. Joy thought their lives sounded
interesting and exciting. She asked many
questions when Ms. Howard finished.

That evening Joy said, "Aunt Nancy, will you please take us to the library?"

"Certainly," said Mrs. Delaney. "What books do you want?"

"Books on Toni Morrison," answered Joy. "And the musicians Duke Ellington and Wynton Marsalis. Ms. Howard told us about all of them today."

Celia and Mrs. Delaney looked at each other and smiled. They were happy something interested Joy.

"Tomorrow's Saturday, so I don't have to work," said Mrs. Delaney. "We'll spend the morning at the library."

"Sounds good, Mom, but can we go to the center first?" said Celia. "I left my good sweater there yesterday."

A crowd was outside the Youth Center on Saturday morning. Everyone was talking at the same time.

"What's going on?" asked Mrs. Delaney and the girls.

"Somebody wrote all over the center's walls," Ms. Howard answered.

"How awful!" exclaimed Joy. "What can we do about it?"

"We're having a meeting in the auditorium now," said Ms. Howard. "Please join us."

When Mrs. Delaney and the girls sat down, the center's director began to speak. "Of course, we'll paint the walls," she said.

"But what about later on?" asked Ms. Howard. "Those who wrote on the walls will do so again."

The director asked for ideas to stop the writing.

Joy waved her hand, but the director didn't see her.

Mrs. Delaney stood and said, "Joy wants to speak."

"Let's paint murals that show important African Americans," said Joy. "Murals will make it hard to write on the walls."

Everyone liked Joy's idea and agreed to paint murals.

First, everyone helped to paint over the writing. Then neighborhood artists drew pictures of the important African Americans everyone had agreed on.

Then everyone helped the artists to paint in the outlined pictures.

Joy worked with others on the mural of Toni Morrison. Celia helped with the mural of Wynton Marsalis. Then they worked together on the mural of Martin Luther King, Jr. One Saturday, Mrs. Delaney worked with them on the mural of Duke Ellington.

"The murals are wonderful," said Mrs. Delaney when they were finished. "The center looks even better than it did before."

"Yes, it does," agreed Ms. Howard. "And I hope people will be too proud of these important African Americans to write on their faces!"

"You're going home in two days, Joy," said
Mrs. Delaney.

"I know," said Joy. "Four weeks went by
quickly."

"I'm sure you'll be back next summer," said
Mrs. Delaney.

"Maybe she won't," said Celia.

Joy smiled and said, "Maybe I will."